A Note from Michelle about WELCOME TO MY ZOO

Hi! I'm Michelle Tanner. I'm nine years old. And my dad finally said I can have a pet of my very own. But instead of picking out just one animal, I wound up taking in *three!* And if anyone finds out, I'll be in big trouble. Now I have to find my extra pets new homes. And I have to keep them a secret from my family, too. But how am I going to do that? My family is huge!

There's my dad and my two older sisters, D.J. and Stephanie. But that's not all.

My mom died when I was little. So my uncle Jesse moved in to help Dad take care of us. So did Joey Gladstone. He's my dad's friend from college. It's almost like having three dads. But that's still not all!

First Uncle Jesse got married to Becky Donaldson. Then they had twin boys, Nicky and Alex. The twins are four years old now. And they're so cute.

That's nine people. And our dog, Comet, makes ten. Sure, it gets kind of crazy sometimes. But I wouldn't change it for anything. It's so much fun living in a full house!

FULL HOUSE™ MICHELLE novels

The Great Pet Project
The Super-Duper Sleepover Party
My Two Best Friends
Lucky, Lucky Day
The Ghost in My Closet
Ballet Surprise
Major League Trouble
My Fourth-Grade Mess
Bunk 3, Teddy and Me
My Best Friend Is a Movie Star! (Super Special)
The Big Turkey Escape
The Substitute Teacher
Calling All Planets
I've Got a Secret
How to Be Cool
The Not-So-Great Outdoors
My Ho-Ho-Horrible Christmas
My Almost Perfect Plan
April Fools!
My Life Is a Three-Ring Circus
Welcome to My Zoo

Activity Book
My Awesome Holiday Friendship Book

Available from MINSTREL Books

FULL HOUSE™
Michelle

Welcome to My Zoo

Jean Waricha

A Parachute Book

A
MINSTREL®
BOOK

Published by POCKET BOOKS
New York   London   Toronto   Sydney   Tokyo   Singapore

This book is a work of fiction. Names, characters, places and incidents are products of the author's imagination or are used fictitiously. Any resemblance to actual events or locales or persons, living or dead, is entirely coincidental.

A MINSTREL PAPERBACK *Original*

 A Minstrel Book published by
POCKET BOOKS, a division of Simon & Schuster Inc.
1230 Avenue of the Americas, New York, NY 10020

A PARACHUTE BOOK

 Copyright © and ™ 1998 by Warner Bros.

FULL HOUSE, characters, names and all related indicia are trademarks of Warner Bros. © 1998.

All rights reserved, including the right to reproduce this book or portions thereof in any form whatsoever. For information address Pocket Books, 1230 Avenue of the Americas, New York, NY 10020

ISBN: 0-671-01731-4

First Minstrel Books printing August 1998

10 9 8 7 6 5 4 3 2 1

A MINSTREL BOOK and colophon are registered trademarks of Simon & Schuster Inc.

Cover photo by Schultz Photography

Printed in the U.S.A.

Welcome to My Zoo

Chapter

1

♥ "I'll get it!" nine-year-old Michelle Tanner shouted. Her strawberry-blond hair bounced as she hurried down the stairs to answer the door. It was a sunny Thursday afternoon. A perfect day for the annual pet parade.

"Hi, come on in," Michelle told her two best friends, Mandy Metz and Cassie Wilkins. "I can't wait to see your new pets!"

Cassie picked up her brand new puppy and Mandy cuddled her brand new pet hamster.

"Can I pet them?" Michelle asked eagerly.

"Sure." Cassie said, holding out the little brown dog.

"What's his name?" Michelle asked as she scratched the puppy behind an ear.

"Shorty," Cassie answered with a big smile. "We named him that because of his stubby legs. He's a dachshund."

Michelle was glad to see her friend so happy. Cassie was sad when her puppy Okay ran away last month.

"And my hamster's name is Melvin," Mandy said.

Michelle patted the fuzzy orange hamster on the head.

"Guess what?" Michelle tickled both of the animals on their bellies. "I've got a friend for you two to meet!

"Come on," Michelle said to Cassie and Mandy. "Let's go find Comet!"

Comet was the Tanner family's dog— a beautiful golden retriever. Michelle had been waiting all week to show him off at the pet parade in the park.

This was the first year Michelle's father, Danny, was letting her take Comet to the parade. And Michelle had been counting the days.

"Now if I can only find that dog," Michelle said.

Cassie placed Shorty on the floor, and Mandy snuggled Melvin close to her cheek. Then the three friends searched the Tanner house for Comet.

"Comet!" Michelle called out. She led Cassie and Mandy and their pets through the kitchen.

"Watch that puppy!" Danny shrieked, grabbing his mop from the sink. "He's getting paw prints all over my clean floor!" Danny rubbed away the tiny smudges.

Cassie picked up Shorty. "Sorry, Mr. Tanner."

"We have to find Comet," Michelle said, searching underneath the table in the center of the room. "And fast."

"Michelle . . ." Danny began.

"Commmmm-ett," Michelle shouted.

"But, Michelle . . ."

"I know," she said quickly. "He's probably in the backyard."

Michelle ran out the kitchen door and into the yard. Her friends followed right behind her. Still no sign of Comet.

"Where could he be?" she wondered out loud.

Danny stepped outside. "That's what I've been trying to tell you, Michelle," he said. "Comet's gone."

"Gone?" Michelle cried. "What do you mean *gone?* What happened to Comet?"

"Calm down, Michelle." Danny patted Michelle on the head. "Nothing's wrong with Comet. He's with Stephanie and Darcy and Allie."

Stephanie was Michelle's thirteen-year-old sister. She was always taking Comet out with her friends, Darcy and Allie. They loved to take him to the park and toss a Frisbee around with him.

Michelle didn't blame Stephanie. Comet was a great dog. The problem was that everyone in the family thought so. And *everyone* wanted to play with him. And that was a lot of people.

Besides her dad and Stephanie, there was Michelle's oldest sister DJ, who was in college. Then there was Michelle's uncle Jesse and aunt Becky, and their two little boys, Nicky and Alex. They all lived on the third floor of the Tanner home.

When Michelle's mom died, Joey Gladstone, her dad's best friend from college, moved in with them to help out. He had an apartment in the basement. Joey was a comedian and was always cracking funny jokes. He loved Comet as much as everyone else in the family.

But today was supposed to be extra special. Today Michelle was supposed to have Comet all to herself.

"But, Dad." Michelle planted her hands on her hips. "You *said* I could take Comet to the pet parade after school today!"

"I forgot!" Danny slapped his hand on his forehead. "I was so busy cleaning the house this morning, I didn't say anything when Stephanie took the dog."

Michelle stared at the floor. She didn't want her dad to see how upset she was. "But you *promised*," she said softly.

"I'm so sorry, pumpkin," Danny brushed the hair out of Michelle's eyes. "But you can still go to the parade without Comet, right?"

Michelle didn't answer. What could she say? What good was going to a pet parade without a pet?

"Come on, Michelle," Mandy said. "It'll be fun."

"Yeah," Cassie added. "You can share *our* pets. You *have* to come with us. Please."

Michelle didn't really want to miss the pet parade. She loved animals. And she didn't want to disappoint her friends. "I guess I'll go," she murmured.

"All right!" Cassie pumped a fist in the air. "You'll have a great time. You'll see!"

"To the pet parade!" Danny raised his mop in the air. "Last one in the car has to finish cleaning the floor!"

The girls raced out the door and piled into Danny's minivan. Shorty jumped on Michelle's lap and licked her face. Michelle giggled and petted the dachshund. Maybe sharing pets at the parade wouldn't be as bad as she thought.

When they arrived at the park, Michelle,

Cassie, and Mandy ran as fast as they could toward the huge line of people and pets.

"We'd better hurry," Mandy shouted, holding Melvin tightly in her arms.

"Yeah," Cassie agreed. "It looks like they're starting!" She picked up Shorty and ran faster.

The parade was even bigger than Michelle had imagined. She saw a very tall man holding a teeny tiny poodle, and a lady with a bird perched on each of her shoulders.

There were dogs, cats, gerbils, mice. . . . Everyone had a pet. Everyone *except* Michelle. She was glad that Cassie and Mandy were sharing their pets with her.

But when the parade began, Cassie grabbed Shorty's leash. Mandy held tightly on to Melvin. And Michelle felt left out.

The parade just wasn't fun without Comet there.

Michelle glanced over the big crowd of people and animals and sighed. I have to find a way to get a pet of my own, she thought. I don't want to share Comet anymore. I need a pet that's all mine!

Chapter

2

♥ "What's the matter, Michelle?" Danny asked at dinner. "Is it my cooking?"

Michelle poked her fork at the pile of green beans in front of her. "No," she muttered.

Michelle listened as Danny, Jesse, Becky, and Joey took turns telling what they did that day. But Michelle didn't want to talk about her day. She didn't want to talk about the parade. She didn't want to talk about anything.

"Maybe you just need some cheering up," Joey said from across the table.

"What did the parakeet say when his owner put sugar in his birdseed?"

"I don't know," Michelle said. "What?"

"This is too *tweet!*" Joey burst out laughing.

Danny, Jesse, and Becky groaned.

Michelle sighed. Joey was usually good at cheering her up—just not today.

"Come on, you guys," Joey said. "My joke wasn't *that* bad."

Uncle Jesse put his hand on Michelle's shoulder. "What's wrong, kiddo?" he asked.

Michelle shrugged.

"You can tell us," Aunt Becky said.

"It's my fault. Isn't it, Michelle?" Danny put down his knife and fork. "I really goofed today." He explained to everyone about the mix-up with Comet.

"I'm sorry, Michelle," Danny said. "I know that sometimes it's hard sharing a pet."

Michelle looked at her father. "Maybe I should get my own pet," she said.

"You know, Michelle," Danny began. "Having your own pet takes a lot of work."

"I know," Michelle replied. "But DJ had a pet turtle before we got Comet. And last year Stephanie had a whole bowl full of goldfish, remember?"

Michelle turned to Jesse and Becky. "Did you guys ever have pets when you were little?"

"Actually, when I was about your age, my parents got me a black Labrador retriever." Jesse smiled. "He was my best friend for a long time."

"I had a little hermit crab named Simon," Becky added.

"Uncle Joey?" Michelle asked. "How about you?"

"A pair of gray ferrets," he admitted.

"Daddy?" Michelle asked.

Danny shook his head. "I never had a pet," he said. "Not until Comet."

"I don't know about that," Joey replied. "Remember that squirrel in college? He always came up to our window in the dorms. And who would feed him nuts?" he asked.

"I would," Danny admitted. "But that squirrel wasn't *really* a pet."

"Didn't you name him?" Joey asked. "Didn't that make him sort of a pet?"

Danny thought for a moment. "I guess so," he said. "Squeaky *was* kind of my pet."

"So everyone had a pet!" Michelle exclaimed.

"Hey, what about us," a voice said.

Michelle felt something tugging at her jeans. She glanced under the table. Nicky and Alex were sitting on the floor by her chair.

Michelle couldn't help but smile. Her

twin cousins were so cute. "I forgot," Michelle said. "Everyone *except* Nicky and Alex."

"But we have our own pet, too," Nicky shouted. "A pet mouse."

"We just got him," Alex added.

Michelle folded her arms across her chest and pouted. "You see," she said. "Even the twins have a pet—and they're only four!"

Becky picked up one of the boys. "The mouse is only—"

"Come on, Dad. Please?" Michelle interrupted. "Can't I have a pet? *Please!*"

"I don't know," Danny replied. "It's a big responsibility. . . . Do you think you can handle it?"

"Yes!" Michelle jumped out of her seat. "I can do it, Dad! I know I can!"

Danny put down his fork and leaned back in his chair. "I'll think about it, Michelle." Then he gave her a little wink.

"Yay!" Michelle cheered. She sat back down and shoved a forkful of green beans in her mouth. *I'll think about it* always meant *yes!*

The next day at school, Michelle couldn't wait to tell all of her friends the good news.

"I'm getting my very own pet!" she told Cassie and Mandy on the playground.

Mandy grabbed Michelle's hands, and the two girls jumped up and down. "That is *so* cool," Mandy shouted.

"What's so cool?" Lucas Hamilton came up to the girls. He was in Michelle's fourth-grade class.

"Michelle's getting a pet," Cassie told him.

"A pet?" Amber Jackson asked, walking past the group. "Who's getting a pet?"

"Michelle is," Lucas told her.

"What kind of pet are you getting, Michelle?" Cassie asked.

"Get a snake!" Lucas yelled. "Snakes are awesome!" He slithered his arm like a snake right in Amber's face. "SSSssssss!"

"Gross!" Amber cried.

Michelle stopped for a second. She had been so caught up in the excitement over just getting a pet, she hadn't even thought about what kind she wanted.

After school Michelle rushed to the library and took out some books on pets. When she got home, the house was very quiet. Michelle stopped long enough to pat Comet on the head. Then she went straight to her room to read.

There are so many different kinds of animals, she thought, picking up a book on guinea pigs. And guinea pigs are one of the coolest. She opened to the first page when the doorbell rang.

Michelle ran downstairs and answered

the door. She was surprised to see her classmate Anna Abdul standing on the porch. Anna's eyes were red. She looked as if she had been crying.

"What's wrong, Anna?" Michelle asked, stepping outside.

Anna pointed to the small metal cage sitting by her feet. "It's my pet bunny rabbit, Snowball," Anna sobbed. "She gives my little brother a rash. And now I have to give her away!"

"She's cute," Michelle said, peeking at the tiny white rabbit in the cage. "What are you going to do with her?"

"Lucas Hamilton told me today in school that you're looking for a pet," Anna replied. "Can you take Snowball?"

"I don't know . . ." Michelle began.

"Snowball's really easy to take care of," Anna said quickly. "And my bunny really needs a new home." She reached into the cage and pulled out the soft, furry rabbit. "Want to hold her?"

Michelle took Snowball into her arms. The bunny looked up at her and twitched its nose. "She's so pretty," Michelle said. Then she rubbed her cheek against Snowball's fur. "And so soft."

It didn't take long for Michelle to decide. "I'll take her," she said. "And you can come over anytime you want to visit."

"Thanks, Michelle!" Anna said. She handed Michelle the rabbit's cage and walked away.

With the bunny still in her arms, Michelle grabbed the cage and went back inside the house. She clicked the door closed with her foot.

Then Michelle remembered something. Something very important.

Dad, she thought. What am I going to tell Dad?

Michelle put down the cage and cuddled

the small, fuzzy animal with both hands. The bunny stared up at Michelle, twitching its little pink nose again.

Michelle smiled. "You're so cute," she said, brushing the soft white fur with her fingers. "And I know Dad's going to let me have a pet. And once he sees you, he'll have to let me keep you . . . right?"

Chapter 3

♥ "Let's get you some carrots," Michelle said to her new pet rabbit. She headed toward the kitchen.

Ding-dong!

"Who could that be? Are you expecting anybody?" Michelle asked her bunny, and giggled.

She put Snowball back into her cage and answered the door. Jonathan Bennett was standing on the porch with a long snake wrapped around his neck. A glass cage sat by his feet. Michelle knew Jonathan from school.

"Whoa," Michelle said, stepping back a little. "Why are you wearing a snake?"

"Lucas Hamilton told me you were looking for a pet," Jonathan said, smiling. "I've had Buddy for two years—ever since he was twelve inches long."

Michelle wasn't sure if she liked snakes. She gazed at the green and brown reptile, and scrunched up her nose. "He looks kind of slimy."

"He's not slimy." Jonathan took the snake off his neck and held him out to Michelle.

Michelle took another step back.

"You're not afraid of snakes, are you?" Jonathan asked her.

"No way!" Michelle said. She reached out and touched Buddy lightly with the tips of her fingers. "Hey," she said, surprised. "His skin is really dry. It feels kind of rough."

"I really want to keep him," Jonathan

began, "but my grandmother is moving in with us. And she's afraid of Buddy. I thought you'd like to have him."

It might be cool to own a snake, Michelle thought. Then she remembered that her dad might let her have one pet—not two.

"He's a good snake," Jonathan added. "He's clean and he's really smart."

"I don't know," Michelle said.

"Please, Michelle," Jonathan begged. "He needs a good home. Look, he likes you."

Michelle watched as Buddy stretched his body closer and closer toward her cheek. The snake flicked out his tongue as if he were trying to give her a little kiss.

Michelle laughed. Maybe she *could* take Buddy. After all, it wouldn't be right to give Snowball a home and turn away Buddy, she thought, just because Snowball showed up first. And her dad always told

Michelle to be fair to everyone. And that included animals . . . right?

"Okay," Michelle said. "I'll take him."

"Great!" Jonathan exclaimed. He put Buddy in his cage and gave him to Michelle.

Michelle carefully carried the glass case into the house. But as soon as she closed the door . . .

Ding-dong!

"I don't believe it!" Michelle cried. "Who is it now?" She put Buddy on the floor and opened the door.

Standing on the porch was a girl about Michelle's age—a beautiful red, blue, and yellow bird sat on her shoulder. Michelle had no idea who the girl was. But Michelle had a feeling she knew what the girl wanted.

"Hi," Michelle said. "Um . . . Who are you?"

"Do you know Lucas Hamilton?" the girl asked.

"Yeah," Michelle replied cautiously. "He's in my class at school."

"Well, I'm his cousin, Gwen." The girl explained. "Lucas—"

"Let me guess," Michelle interrupted. "He told you I was looking for a pet, right?"

"How did you know?" the girl asked.

Michelle couldn't help but laugh. "Lucas told everybody!" She motioned to her two new pets in the living room. "I'm sorry," Michelle continued, "but I can't take your bird. My dad would *never* let me keep *three* pets!"

Suddenly she heard another voice.

"Never let me keep *three* pets!"

"Who said that?" Michelle asked.

"Who said that?" the voice repeated.

Michelle looked around.

"That's just my parrot, Polly," Gwen

24

said, pointing to the bird on her shoulder. "She talks!"

"Wow!" Michelle said.

"Polly can sound like anything. An alarm clock, a TV announcer . . . *any-thing!*"

"Anything!" the bird repeated.

"That's so cool!" Michelle exclaimed.

Before she knew it, Michelle was standing inside her living room with a pet parrot on her shoulder and a bird cage in her hand.

"Why did I say I would take her?" Michelle groaned after Gwen left. "What was I thinking?"

That morning Michelle wanted one pet. But now she had three!

"I'm sorry, guys," she said to the pets. "I can't keep all of you."

But Michelle didn't know which one to pick. Each animal was special in its own way. She stared at the fluffy bunny, the cool snake, and the smart parrot. "Which one should I keep? It's impossible to decide."

Michelle leaned over and rubbed her cheek against the fuzzy white bunny. "I think I'll keep you," she said to Snowball.

Out of the three pets, Snowball was the closest thing to a guinea pig. And that *was* the pet she wanted in the first place.

"As soon as Dad says I can have a pet," she told the rabbit. "I'll introduce you to my whole family. Everyone is going to love you!"

"I'll find you both great new homes," she told Buddy and Polly. "But first I have to think of a place to hide all of you."

But where? she wondered. Under her bed? Michelle shook her head at the idea. Dad dusts under there at least twice a week. He'd find them right away.

My closet? Michelle thought. No. Too crowded . . . *and* too dark.

"I know," she said aloud. "I'll hide you in the garage!"

Michelle quickly carried the three animals out of the house. She placed the cages on a table all the way in the back. Then she pulled out an old sign she made last year when she was working on her science project.

SCIENTIST AT WORK IN GARAGE
DO **NOT** COME IN HERE!

"That should keep everybody out," Michelle whispered. "I hope!"

Chapter 4

♥ After hanging her sign, Michelle skipped all the way to the kitchen. I have to take good care of all the animals, she thought. Until I find them a nice home.

She opened the refrigerator and peered inside. I'll get some carrots for Snowball first, she thought. Then I'll look in my books to find out what snakes and parrots like to eat.

Michelle grabbed a big bag of carrots from the refrigerator and closed the door.

"Michelle, where are you going with that?" Danny said.

"Dad!" Michelle said, dropping the bag on the floor. She turned around. "Uh . . . what are you doing home so soon?"

Danny smiled. "I came home early because I have a surprise for you."

Michelle saw that he was holding something behind his back. "All right!" Michelle jumped up and down. "A surprise!"

"Now close your eyes. . . ."

Michelle did exactly as her father said.

"Okay," Danny said. "Open them!"

Michelle opened her eyes wide. Her father was holding a small metal cage with a big red bow tied around it. "What is it?" she asked.

"Take a closer look," Danny replied.

Michelle peered into the cage. Sleeping in the corner was a tiny animal with shiny black fur. "A guinea pig!" Michelle shouted, clapping her hands together.

"He's yours!" Danny exclaimed.

Michelle couldn't believe her eyes.

"How did you know Dad?" she asked him. "How did you know that I wanted a guinea pig?"

"Actually," Danny admitted, "I've always wanted one, ever since I was a little kid. I thought you might like one, too."

"I do!" Michelle hugged her dad. "Thank you! Thank you! Thank you!"

Danny placed the cage on the counter. Then he showed Michelle how to take care of the animal.

"Well, I'll leave you and your new pet alone," Danny said when he finished. "But remember, Michelle, taking care of him is a big responsibility."

Bigger than you think, she said to herself. Michelle's shoulders sagged. Now I have four pets! What am I going to do?

Maybe I should just tell Dad about the others, she thought. But then he might not let me keep the guinea pig. He might say that I wasn't responsible enough to take care of it. There's no way I can tell him, she decided. No way!

"I know it's a big responsibility, Dad," she said to him. "And I'll take good care of my new pet. Don't worry."

"Great," Danny said, turning to leave. "Oh, and, Michelle . . . pick up those carrots, will you?"

After her father was gone, Michelle cleaned up the mess she had made. She carried her new guinea pig to her bedroom. Then she rushed out to the garage.

"I'm sorry, Snowball," she told the bunny as it munched on the carrots. "I'm going to have to find a new home for you, too."

Later, Michelle looked through her pet books. She found out that parrots like to eat sunflower seeds. She found a bag of them in the kitchen cupboard and fed some to Polly. One book said that a lot of snakes eat mice! Michelle thought that was gross, so she fed Buddy pieces of bread instead.

For the rest of the afternoon, Michelle sat in the garage and played with Snowball, Buddy, and Polly. She tried to figure out how to find new homes for them. But she couldn't come up with a single idea.

At dinner, Michelle was very quiet. She still didn't have a plan. But she had decided to ask Mandy and Cassie for help tomorrow.

At least my secret is safe, she thought. No one will go into the garage. My Scientist-at-Work sign will take care of that.

"So, Michelle," Danny said after he swallowed a mouth full of peas. "What have you been up to?"

"Uh . . . nothing," she said.

"You've been in the garage all day," Danny replied. "You must have been doing *something*."

"Yeah," Stephanie added, picking up a

forkful of mashed potatoes. "What's with the sign on the garage door?"

Michelle gulped. She had to think fast.

"I'm working on a school project," she answered quickly.

"What kind of project?" Danny asked her.

"Uhhh," Michelle stuttered, "I—I'm doing an experiment with . . . with . . ." She looked down at her plate. The only thing left on it were three icky pieces of broccoli. "With vegetables!" she answered.

"Ohhh," Danny said. "So that's what you were doing with that bag of carrots."

Michelle let out a deep breath. "Yup. For the science fair."

"But the fair at your school was *last* month," Stephanie chimed in. "Why are you doing a science project now?"

"Ummmm . . ." Michelle had to say something quick. "Ummmm . . . extra credit?"

"That's wonderful, Michelle!" Danny exclaimed.

Whew, Michelle thought. That was close. "Can I be excused?" she asked. "I need to check my . . . uh . . . project in the garage."

"Go ahead," Danny said.

Michelle jumped up and headed for the door.

"Oh, Michelle," Danny said. "I forgot to tell you something."

Michelle froze. "What is it, Dad?" she asked.

"I'm planning to clean the garage on Sunday," he answered. "So you'll have to move your science stuff somewhere else by Saturday night, okay?"

Michelle gulped. It was already Friday night. That meant she had just *one* day to figure out what to do with *three* pets!

Chapter
5

♥ "I'm in big trouble," Michelle whispered when Cassie and Mandy came over the next afternoon. She led the girls into the garage and closed the door.

"This is Snowball, Polly, and Buddy." Michelle pointed to the cages. Then she explained her problem.

"And the worst part is my dad's going to clean in here Sunday morning," she said, flopping on the floor near the pets. "He told me I have to have my stuff out of here by Saturday night."

"That's tonight!" Mandy exclaimed.

"I know," Michelle said. She pulled Snowball out of her cage and patted the bunny on the head. "Do you guys have any ideas?"

Cassie and Mandy shrugged.

"Hey," Michelle said after a minute. "We could take the animals around the neighborhood and ask if anybody wants them."

"That's a great idea!" Mandy said as she watched Polly eat a sunflower seed.

"Don't worry, Michelle," Cassie said. "We'll help you find homes for them."

"I wish we knew where to start," Michelle said. "There's got to be somebody we know who's looking for a pet."

The girls grew silent.

"I got it!" Mandy shouted suddenly. "My neighbor Mr. Potter! He lives alone. And he spends all day in his vegetable garden talking to his plants. I bet he'd love a pet!"

"And I'm sure Snowball would be happy living in a place were there are lots of carrots," Michelle added.

"Do you think he'd want a bunny?" Cassie asked.

"There's only one way to find out," Michelle said. "And if he doesn't want Snowball, he might want one of the other animals. Let's go to Mr. Potter's!"

The three friends gathered up the pets and their cages. Michelle picked up Snowball. Cassie took hold of Polly. And Mandy held on to Buddy.

When they arrived at Mr. Potter's house, Michelle found him in his garden. He was picking bugs off a head of lettuce.

"Excuse me, Mr. Potter," Michelle said, holding Snowball in her cage. "We're trying to find these pets a new home."

"What a nice thing to do!" Mr. Potter exclaimed. He gazed at the animals in the cages. Then he stuck his finger inside

Snowball's cage. "She's a cute one, isn't she?"

Snowball twitched her pink little nose, and sniffed Mr. Potter's finger.

"Snowball likes you, Mr. Potter," Cassie said.

"And I like her, too," Mr. Potter replied. "And I certainly have enough food to feed this little bunny," he added, motioning to his vegetable garden. "I'd be delighted to give Snowball a new home."

"That's great!" Michelle said, handing Snowball over to Mr. Potter. "Snowball's a good bunny. You won't be sorry."

"One down, two to go," Michelle announced as she, Cassie and Mandy left Mr. Potter's house. This doesn't seem too hard, she thought, walking down the sidewalk.

"Look!" Mandy said. She pointed to Mrs. Dibble sitting on her front porch with a tiny brown dog.

"But Mrs. Dibble already has a pet," Cassie said. "Don't you see her holding her little Chihuahua, Chips?"

Michelle watched Mrs. Dibble rocking back and forth on her chair with Chips on her lap. Then she saw the woman put her hand into a brown paper bag and throw something onto her front lawn. A flock of birds flew over to eat what Mrs. Dibble had given them.

Michelle smiled. "Mrs. Dibble sure does like birds."

"Yes, she does," Mandy said. "She even goes on bird-watching trips all around the country."

"If Mrs. Dibble likes birds so much, why doesn't she have one?" Cassie asked. She moved Polly's cage to her other hand.

"She told me that she was looking for a really special bird," Mandy replied.

Michelle smiled. "I know a bird that's really special," she said.

"Me, too," Cassie said. "One that talks!"

Michelle, Mandy, and Cassie brought Polly to Mrs. Dibble's porch.

"Hello, girls," Mrs. Dibble said. "What a beautiful bird."

"Beautiful bird," Polly repeated.

Mrs. Dibble smiled with delight.

"She talks," Cassie said.

"I can hear that," Mrs. Dibble said, laughing.

"Polly's really great," Mandy said. "But Michelle has to give her away. She has too many pets."

"Do you think you'd like her?" Michelle asked. "She's very smart!"

"Well, I've been looking for a feathered friend for my dog, Chips, for the longest time." Mrs. Dibble took the bird cage from Cassie. She reached inside and petted Polly. "What a pretty bird," she said.

"Pretty bird," Polly repeated.

Mrs. Dibble smiled. "I'll take her!"

"Thanks, Mrs. Dibble!" Michelle said. "You won't be sorry!"

Michelle was feeling better and better. Only one pet left to find a good home for.

But she knew that finding a snake a home wasn't going to be easy.

The girls brought Buddy to five different houses. Nobody wanted him. Even worse, it was almost dinnertime. And Michelle had to go home soon.

"Nobody's ever going to take Buddy." Mandy frowned. She placed the snake's tank on the ground, and sat down beside it.

"Come on, you guys," Michelle said. "Don't give up now. We're so close."

"It's all Lucas Hamilton's fault." Cassie plopped down on the sidewalk. "If he didn't tell everybody that you were looking for a pet, we'd never be in this mess."

Michelle sat down next to her friends. "You're right," she said. "But I didn't have to take *all* of the pets either. It's my fault, too."

"If only we knew someone weird enough to like snakes." Cassie plopped down on the sidewalk, too. "Uh . . . aside from you, Michelle."

"Thanks a lot." Michelle gave Mandy a friendly punch on the arm.

The three girls sat silently, thinking.

Michelle thought really hard. Who would want a snake?

Then she jumped up.

"I can't believe I didn't think of this earlier," she said. "It's perfect!"

"What?" Cassie and Mandy asked at the same time.

"Lucas Hamilton," Michelle replied.

"He told me I should get a snake, remember? He thinks they're awesome!"

"You're right!" Cassie said, bouncing to her feet. "Do you think his mom would let him have a snake?"

"Let's go find out!" Michelle cried.

Michelle, Cassie, and Mandy raced to Lucas's house. When they got there, Michelle rang the bell and Lucas answered the door.

"Oh, cool!" Lucas said, eyeing Buddy in his glass case. "You got a snake!"

"Yeah," Michelle said. "But my dad bought me a guinea pig, so I have to give him away."

"We thought you might like him," Mandy chimed in.

"Oh, cool!" Lucas said again, and ran into his house. "Mom!"

A few minutes later, Lucas and Mrs. Hamilton came to the door.

"See, Mom," Lucas said. "He's not gross."

Mrs. Hamilton nodded. "I don't want it messing up my house, Lucas," she said.

"Jonathan Bennett told me that snakes are very clean animals," Michelle said.

"And he'll stay in his cage?" Mrs. Hamilton asked.

"Sure, Mom. I promise," Lucas said. "Can I keep him, Mom? Please, can I?"

Mrs. Lucas sighed. "Okay."

"Yes!" Lucas pumped his fist in the air. Then he took the cage. "Thanks, Michelle!"

The girls said good-bye to Lucas and Buddy and headed home. Michelle was so glad that Mrs. Hamilton let Lucas keep Buddy. She let out a huge cheer as she and her friends skipped away.

That night, when Michelle went to bed, she felt great! She had found three wonderful homes for the animals. And best of all, Michelle was able to keep her own pet.

What should I name him? she wondered as she drifted off into a restful sleep.

The next morning, Michelle woke up early and got dressed. She tiptoed over to her guinea pig, and peeked into his cage.

"Good morning," Michelle sang to him. She opened the tiny door and scooped her new pet into her hands. "I still don't know what to call you," she told him. "It has to be a special name."

She bounced down the stairs to the living room, petting his shiny black fur. "Maybe Cassie or Mandy will have an idea for your name," she told him.

Brrrinnnggg!

"Maybe that's them now," Michelle picked up the phone. "Hello?" she said into the receiver.

"I've got a big problem," a voice said frantically on the other end of the line. "I don't know what to do!"

It was Mrs. Dibble, the woman who had taken Polly, the parrot.

"What is it, Mrs. Dibble?" Michelle asked. "What's wrong?"

"Just come over, Michelle," she cried. "You've got to get over here right away!"

Chapter
6

♥ Michelle rushed right over to Mrs. Dibble's house. It didn't take long for her to understand why the woman was so upset. Polly and Mrs. Dibble's tiny Chihuahua, Chips, were having a barking match.

"Yipe! Yipe! Yipe!" The two animals kept barking at each other.

"They've been going at it all night and all morning!" Mrs. Dibble cried. "I don't know how to stop them!"

Polly had learned to make a high-pitched yelp, just like the little dog's. And

Chips was going crazy trying to out-bark her.

"Yipe! Yipe! Yipe! Yipe! Yipe!" Chips barked again.

"Yipe! Yipe! Yipe! Yipe! Yipe!" Polly cried.

"Hush, Chips. Hush," Mrs. Dibble shouted.

After a moment the little dog stopped yapping. Then Mrs. Dibble turned to Michelle.

"You've got to take the parrot back," Mrs. Dibble said. "I just can't live with all this noise."

Michelle's heart sank.

Chips began yelping again.

"Yipe! Yipe! Yipe! Yipe! Yipe! Yipe!" Polly replied.

"Please take this noisy bird out of here!" Mrs. Dibble cried, covering her ears with her hands. Then she handed Michelle the bird cage.

"But I can't take her home," Michelle tried to explain. "Not now. Not after—"

"I'm sorry." Mrs. Dibble gently pushed Michelle and Polly out of the house. "Good-bye," she said.

"Good-bye," Polly called back as Mrs. Dibble closed the door.

Michelle sat down on the steps in front of the house. "You are such a noisy bird," she said to Polly. "You have to learn to be quiet."

"Be quiet," the bird repeated.

Michelle looked at Polly. Wait a minute, she said to herself.

"Be quiet," Michelle said again.

"Be quiet," Polly called back.

Michelle jumped to her feet and rang Mrs. Dibble's doorbell.

"I thought I told you to take that noisy bird away," Mrs. Dibble scolded when she opened the door.

"I have an idea," Michelle explained to her. "And I think it will solve *both* of our problems."

Michelle stepped inside and set the bird cage down. "What did you say to make Chips stop barking before?" Michelle asked.

"I always say, 'Hush, Chips. Hush,'" she answered.

"Hush, Chips. Hush," Polly repeated.

Mrs. Dibble looked at Michelle and smiled.

"Let's test it out." Michelle cleared her throat. Then she tried to bark just like Chips.

Polly stared at Michelle.

"Hush, Chips. Hush," Mrs. Dibble said.

"Hush, Chips. Hush," Polly repeated.

Michelle and Mrs. Dibble cheered.

"Now for the *real* test," Michelle said. She searched the floor for the little Chihuahua. "Chips," she called. "Here, boy!"

The tiny dog bolted into the room. He headed straight for Polly's cage, yipping loudly.

Michelle held her breath. Chips kept barking and barking.

"Hush, Chips. Hush," Polly answered.

Chips cocked his head, and stopped yelping.

"Hush, Chips. Hush," Polly said again.

Michelle couldn't believe it. Her idea really worked. "Will you give Polly another chance?" she asked Mrs. Dibble.

"Well, she's such a beautiful bird . . . and clever, too." Mrs. Dibble smiled. "Okay, Polly," she said to the bird. "You get another chance!"

Michelle sighed with relief. Then she thanked Mrs. Dibble, and ran all the way home.

"At last," she said when she reached her front door, "I can play with my guinea pig."

But when Michelle got inside the house, Danny stopped her. "Cassie and Mandy are here to see you," he told her. "They're in the kitchen, eating some of my new chocolate-covered cherry cookies."

"Great," Michelle said. She gave her father a quick kiss on the cheek. Then she ran into the kitchen, with Danny right behind her.

"And Mr. Potter called you twice," Danny continued. "Something about his new pet rabbit . . ."

Michelle froze. "His new pet rabbit?"

"Yes," Danny replied.

"Um . . . thanks, Dad," Michelle said as calmly as she could. She wondered what Mr. Potter was calling about. She hoped it was good news.

As soon as her father left, Michelle dialed Mr. Potter's number on the kitchen phone. Cassie and Mandy stood silently by her side.

"Hi, Mr. Potter, it's Michelle Tanner," she said into the phone.

Mr. Potter's voice cracked on the other line. "I've got a big problem, Michelle," he said frantically. "And you have to get over here right away!"

Chapter

7

♥ "What's wrong, Mr. Potter?" Michelle gasped for breath. She and her friends ran the whole way to Mr. Potter's house.

Mr. Potter led Michelle, Mandy, and Cassie out the back door to his vegetable garden. "Look!" He pointed to the tiny white bunny munching on his freshly grown carrots. "That fur ball is ruining my garden!"

Mr. Potter bounded over to Snowball, and swiped her up from the ground. "Here," he said to Michelle, shoving the rabbit into her arms. "I don't want to see this bunny around here again!"

Michelle sighed. What else could go wrong today?

Snowball started wriggling in her hands. The rabbit let out a little squeal and broke free. She dashed toward a patch of ripe red tomatoes.

"No!" Michelle cried, and raced after the rabbit. Then Cassie and Mandy tried to grab her. But Snowball bolted away!

Mandy stumbled forward.

"Watch my tomatoes!" Mr. Potter yelped. He threw his hands over his eyes.

But Mandy couldn't keep her balance. She landed face first, right into the patch.

Michelle and Cassie rushed over to Mandy.

Mandy stood up. "I'm okay," she said, trying to brush off the wet, crushed tomatoes.

Mr. Potter groaned. "My poor carrots!

My poor tomatoes!" He gazed into his garden. "My lettuce!" he shrieked. "Look! That rabbit is destroying my beautiful lettuce leaves now!"

"We'll get Snowball!" Michelle cried. She chased the bunny around the yard, but she couldn't catch her. Snowball was too fast.

Then Michelle got an idea. She grabbed a carrot and showed it to Snowball. She hoped the bunny would come over to eat it. But Snowball was happily munching on a piece of lettuce.

"It's not working." Michelle sighed. "Snowball's not going to come over for a carrot."

"Get her, Michelle," Mandy whispered. "Now, while she's not looking!"

Michelle lunged for the rabbit, but Snowball was too quick. She slipped right out of Michelle's hands.

"I'm never going to be able to grab her," Michelle moaned. "We have to think of a way to get Snowball to come to us."

She thought for a minute. "I wonder what else rabbits like?" she asked aloud. "Besides vegetables."

"How about another rabbit?" Cassie asked. "You know, like a friend."

"Hmmmm. Maybe that *would* work." Michelle nodded her head up and down.

Mr. Potter shook his head from side to side. "No way, Michelle," he said. "I can't handle one rabbit. I'm not about to deal with two."

"Hmmmm." Michelle glanced over at Snowball's empty cage. Then she snapped her fingers. "How about using a mirror instead of another rabbit? We'll make Snowball *think* another bunny is around."

"Keep your eyes on that rabbit," Mr.

57

Potter said, running toward his house. "I'll be right back." He returned a few seconds later with a mirror. Mr. Potter handed it to Michelle.

Michelle knelt in the middle of the vegetable patch, and placed the mirror on the thick green grass. "Snowball!" she called. "Here, bunny!"

Snowball looked at the mirror and tilted her head.

"Snowball's trying to figure out who the other rabbit is," Cassie said excitedly. "She doesn't know it's her!"

The bunny slowly hopped toward the mirror.

With every hop, Michelle backed up toward the rabbit's cage, pulling the mirror with her.

Snowball followed her reflection.

"It's working," Mandy whispered.

Michelle backed up some more . . . and

some more. When she was close enough to the cage, she leaned the mirror against it. Then she scooped up Snowball, and put her inside.

Mr. Potter quickly locked the wire door. "You did it!" he shouted gleefully. "You got Snowball back into her cage!"

"I'm sorry Snowball ruined your garden, Mr. Potter," Michelle said.

"It's okay, Michelle," he told her. "Now that I think about it . . . maybe it was *my* fault. I might have left the latch open."

"Does that mean you'll let Snowball stay?" Michelle asked.

"I don't know," Mr. Potter said, scooping Snowball out of her cage. "She caused a lot of trouble. . . ." He cuddled the bunny next to his cheek. "But I guess it's only fair to give her another chance. Especially if I left the cage unlocked.

"Okay," Mr. Potter said, smiling.

"Snowball gets another chance. Maybe next week I'll even build her a bigger house."

The three girls cheered.

"Whoa! Two close calls in one day," Michelle said to her friends as they walked back to the Tanner house.

"But the important thing is that Mrs. Dibble and Mr. Potter are keeping their pets, right?" Cassie replied.

"We're just lucky that Lucas is crazy about snakes," Mandy said. "He'll never want to give Buddy back."

When the girls turned the corner, Michelle saw Mrs. Hamilton running toward them. She was waving her hands over her head.

"I have a bad feeling about this," Michelle said to her friends.

"I've been calling you all afternoon," Mrs. Hamilton cried when she reached the girls. "Your father told me you might be at Mr. Potter's."

"Let me guess," Michelle said. "You have a big problem. And I've got to get over there right away, right?"

"Yes," Mrs. Hamilton replied. "How did you know?"

Chapter

8

♥ "This way." Mrs. Hamilton led the girls through her house. She stopped just long enough to rub a few fingerprints off her sparkling dining room table.

Dad would love this place, Michelle thought, walking into the living room. The couch and chairs were covered with clear plastic. The wooden coffee table was shiny and polished. And the white carpet was totally spotless!

Lucas was kneeling over Buddy, his eyes red and watery. "You gave me a sick snake!" he told Michelle.

"Buddy does look strange." Michelle crouched down to get a better look at the animal. "It looks like he's peeling!"

"And his skin is getting all over my carpet," Mrs. Hamilton complained. "You told me snakes were clean animals!"

Mandy leaned closer to Michelle. "What do we do?" she asked.

Michelle reached out to touch some of the snake's skin on the rug.

"Be careful, Michelle," Cassie warned her. "You might catch whatever it has!"

Michelle pulled her hand back. Then she remembered something she read in one of her pet books. Michelle laughed and picked up a big piece of skin. "Buddy's just shedding," she said.

"Is that *normal*?" Lucas asked.

"Of course it is," Michelle answered. "All snakes have to shed their skin. When they grow bigger, they need bigger skin," Michelle explained. "So, they shed the old stuff."

"I thought you really liked snakes," Mandy said to Lucas. "How come you didn't know that?"

"I *do* like snakes," Lucas replied. "I just don't know anything about them yet."

Michelle let out a big sigh of relief. "Well, at least that's over with." She stood up. "I'll see you in school, Lucas."

"Not so fast, Michelle," Mrs. Hamilton said. "I don't want that snake shedding all over my carpet. You'll have to take him back."

"But Mom!" Lucas cried.

"No buts," Mrs. Hamilton said. "I told you I wanted an animal that didn't make a mess. . . ."

Michelle's shoulders sagged. "It's okay, Mrs. Hamilton. I'll take him back."

Michelle placed the peeling snake into the glass tank and headed for the door.

"What are you going to do with Buddy?" Mandy asked on the way back to Michelle's house. "Your dad's cleaning the garage today. So you can't hide the snake in there."

"I know," Michelle said. "I have to sneak him back into my house. *And* I have nowhere to put him!"

When they got to Michelle's house, Michelle gave the snake to Cassie. Then she peeked in through her front door and tiptoed inside.

"What luck," she whispered to herself, looking around the quiet house. "Nobody's home." Michelle waved to her friends. "The coast is clear, you guys. Bring in Buddy."

Cassie tucked the snake's glass tank in a corner next to a chair. Then she took

Buddy out and sat on the couch to play with him. "He's kind of cool," she said as Buddy twirled around her arm.

"I'll be right back," Michelle called, and headed toward the kitchen. "I'll get us some drinks."

Mandy followed her.

Michelle grabbed three sodas out of the refrigerator. She handed one to Mandy.

"Can we have some more of your dad's chocolate-covered cherry cookies?" Cassie asked, swinging open the kitchen door.

"Sure," Michelle said. She closed the refrigerator and looked on the countertop for the cookies.

"Wait a minute . . ." Michelle turned around. "Uh . . . Cassie? Where's the snake?"

"I left him on the couch," Cassie replied.

"On the couch?" Michelle shouted. "But he could get away!"

"He looked really comfortable," Cassie cried.

Michelle rushed back into the living room. She raced over to the sofa.

Buddy was gone!

Chapter

9

♥ "Buddy's loose in the house," Michelle cried. "We have to find him!"

Michelle, Cassie, and Mandy searched the entire living room for the snake—with no luck.

"The couch," Michelle ordered. "Maybe he's hiding *under* it."

Michelle got down on her hands and knees and peeked under one end of the couch. Mandy and Cassie looked under the other side. The snake was nowhere to be found.

Bam!

"Uh-oh," Michelle whispered. She knew that noise. Someone had come in the front door.

"Michelle?" Danny called. "What are you doing?"

Michelle looked up. Her father stood over her, with Nicky and Alex beside him.

Michelle didn't know what to tell him. She couldn't say that they were looking for a lost snake. Then she'd have to explain the whole story.

"Uh . . . we were cleaning!" Michelle announced.

"You were what?" A big smile spread across Danny's face. "I never thought I'd see the day when you *wanted* to clean the house. This calls for a celebration. I'm going to bake some more cookies!"

Michelle shrugged her shoulders and smiled. "Come on," she said to her friends. "Let's go clean my room now."

"Whew," Mandy said as they headed up the stairs. "That was close . . . again."

Michelle stopped. "What was that?" she whispered. "I think I heard a hissing sound."

"I heard it, too," Cassie said.

Michelle gazed up the stairs. The snake was slithering to the second floor. "It's Buddy," she whispered, running up the steps. "We have to get him!"

Michelle and her friends charged for the snake. But Buddy was too fast. He slithered away quickly—out of sight.

"Where did he go?" Mandy asked when they reached the second floor landing.

"Shhh," Michelle said. She stood silently, listening for the snake. Then she heard it.

"The hissing noise," Michelle said. "I think it's coming from the third floor."

The girls raced up another flight of

stairs. "It's coming from Nicky and Alex's room," Cassie whispered.

As they stepped inside the twins' room, the snake slithered under Nicky's bed.

"Here, Buddy," Michelle called as she crawled underneath the bed. She stretched her arm toward the snake and he neatly slid around it. "Got him!" she cried.

Michelle scrambled out from under the bed with Buddy wrapped around her arm.

"Let's put him in here for now," Michelle said, placing Buddy in the basket under her desk when they reached her bedroom.

"Hey. I like your guinea pig," Cassie said, staring into the cage on Michelle's desk. "What's his name?"

Michelle shook her head. "I've been so busy worrying about all the other animals, I haven't even had time to name him."

"Oh, no!" Mandy cried.

"Don't worry, Mandy. It's no big deal.

I'll think of a name for him soon," Michelle said.

"No, not that!" Mandy exclaimed. "We left Buddy's tank in the living room! We have to get it before your dad finds it!"

The girls rushed down the stairs. Michelle could hear Danny humming in the kitchen. Just as Michelle picked up Buddy's tank, the doorbell rang.

"I'll get it," Michelle called to her father. She put down the tank and opened the door. "Mr. Potter!" she gasped.

Mr. Potter stood in the doorway. He held up a half-eaten zucchini in one hand and Snowball the bunny in the other.

"Oh, no!" Michelle groaned.

"She got into the garden again," Mr. Potter said. "And this time I'm sure that I locked the door to her cage."

He held out the wire cage with the little white rabbit inside. "I'm sorry, Michelle. But I can't keep Snowball."

Michelle sighed and took the bunny. She hadn't even closed the door when Mrs. Dibble marched onto the porch.

"You have to take this parrot back," Mrs. Dibble announced.

"Did Polly and Chips get into another barking match?" Cassie asked, peeking over Michelle's shoulder.

The old woman shook her head. "Everything's great between Chips and Polly," she said. "But now Polly's imitating the telephone. It's driving me nuts!"

Mrs. Dibble handed Michelle the colorful bird and walked away.

"This can't be happening!" Michelle cried. "I have all the pets back again! What am I going to do with them?"

"Michelle," Danny called from the kitchen. "Come on in here. The cookies are almost ready."

"What am I going to do?" Michelle moaned.

"Put them in the garage," Cassie suggested.

"I can't," Michelle said. "My dad is going to clean it today, remember?"

"That's right. I forgot," Cassie said. "Well, let's hide them in your room for now."

"Michelle!" Danny called again.

"And we'd better do it fast!" Mandy added.

Cassie and Mandy helped Michelle hide the animals in her room. Then they headed for the kitchen.

Nicky and Alex sat at the table, each with an uneaten cookie in front of them. They were both crying.

"What's the matter?" Michelle asked the twins. "Why are you crying?"

Nicky wiped the tears from his eyes and struggled to get the words out of his mouth. "We . . . we went up to our room before . . . and we couldn't find our pet mouse!"

Michelle gulped. Then she glanced over at Cassie and Mandy. She knew her friends were thinking the same thing she was.

They had found the snake in the twins' room.

Michelle suddenly felt sick.

Did Buddy eat the twins' mouse?

Chapter

10

♥ Michelle, Cassie, and Mandy ran to the twins' room to search for the mouse.

"Maybe it's just lost," Michelle cried. "We have to find it!"

Mandy looked under the twins' beds. Cassie looked inside the closet.

But there was no sign of the mouse.

"Keep looking!" Michelle begged, checking behind the dresser.

"Michelle, can you come down here?" her father called.

"In a minute, Dad. Okay?" Michelle yelled back. I have to keep looking for the twins' mouse, she thought. I can't stop until I find it.

"No, not in a minute. *Now!*" Danny insisted.

When Michelle entered the kitchen, her heart almost stopped. Danny stood in front of the sink. In one hand he held a head of lettuce, in the other, a furry white bunny.

"Would you happen to know anything about this rabbit?" Michelle's dad asked. "The boys don't."

Michelle didn't answer at first. "Well, it all started—"

Beep! Beep! Beep! Beep!

Danny handed the rabbit to Michelle. He ran to the oven and pulled out a batch of black, smoking cookies. "I forgot about these," he groaned.

Beep! Beep! Beep! Beep!

"What's that noise?" Michelle shouted.

"It's the smoke detector," Danny answered. "My burnt cookies set it off." He marched over to the alarm and pulled it off the wall. "I'll put these back when I'm finished baking," he said, removing the batteries.

Joey ran into the kitchen. "I was taking a nap downstairs, when I heard the fire alarm. Is anything burning?"

"Just my cookies," Danny said. "But—"

Beep! Beep! Beep! Beep!

"Oh, no. One of the smoke alarms is going off upstairs, too," Danny said. "Come on, guys. Help me find which one it is." He turned to Michelle. "Then we'll talk about the rabbit."

Danny led the group into the living room just as Jesse and Becky walked through the front door.

"What's going on in here?" Jessie shouted over the beeping noise.

"I'm trying to find out which smoke alarm is going off," Danny told them.

"We lost our mouse! We lost our mouse!" The twins ran over to their parents.

Jesse picked up both of them. "Don't worry, kids," he said. "We'll find him."

"Hey! Nice rabbit," Jesse turned to Michelle. "Where did you get her?"

Beep! Beep! Beep! Beep!

"Forget about that rabbit," Danny said. "Help me find the smoke alarm. It's giving me a headache."

Everyone followed Danny up the stairs.

"It sounds like it's coming from the second floor," Danny said as he reached the top of the landing. "This is weird." Danny frowned, checking the smoke alarm in the hallway. "This one isn't beeping."

Beep! Beep! Beep! Beep!

79

"Wait a minute." Danny listened. "It sounds like it's coming from Michelle's room."

Danny marched down the hall and stepped inside her room.

"Michelle!" He gasped. "How are you going to explain *this*?"

Chapter

11

♥ "Uh-oh." Michelle stepped inside her room. Polly was perched on top of her dresser.

"Beep! Beep! Beep! Beep!" the parrot chirped.

Buddy was slithering up Michelle's bed.

"Where did all these animals come from?" Danny cried.

Michelle smiled at him weakly. She glanced from the bunny in her arms, to the snake, to the parrot, and back to her father. She could feel her face turning red.

Then she explained everything. How

Lucas Hamilton told everyone that she was looking for a pet. How she just couldn't say no to all the animals. And how she tried to find homes for them.

"I just wanted my own pet," Michelle said. "But I got four pets instead. And when I tried to give the bunny, parrot, and snake away . . . everything got messed up!

"And that's not the worst part!" Michelle glanced at Cassie, then at Mandy. Then she looked at her two cousins.

"What could be worse?" Danny's eyebrows shot way up.

Michelle didn't answer.

"Whatever it is," Uncle Jesse said. "You can tell us."

Michelle sat on her bed. She took a deep breath and began. "I think Buddy might have eaten the twins' mouse."

The room fell silent. Then everyone burst into laughter.

"What's so funny?" Michelle asked.

Danny put his arm around Michelle, and laughed some more. "Why don't you tell her, Becky."

Becky smiled and pulled out an old white sock from her coat pocket. It had eyes, a nose, a mouth, and two little mouse ears on top.

"This is Nicky and Alex's pet mouse," she said putting her hand inside the sock. "I forgot I had it in my pocket."

Michelle let out a huge sigh of relief. "Are you still mad at me, Daddy?" Michelle asked, lowering her head.

Danny sat on Michelle's bed, and gave her a kiss on the forehead. "No, pumpkin," he answered. "I'm not angry. I understand how you couldn't say no to your friends," he continued. "But sometimes saying no is the right thing to do."

"I guess you're right," Michelle said. "But we still have to figure out what to do with my extra pets." Michelle shook her head. "Finding them homes didn't exactly work out."

"Why don't we have an adopt-a-pet party next weekend?" Danny suggested after a moment.

"Yay, a party!" Nicky and Alex jumped up and down.

"That's a great idea," Aunt Becky agreed.

Michelle nodded. "That way we don't have to find people who want pets. They'll come to us!"

"And we won't give a pet to someone unless we're sure they'll love it and take care of it no matter what," Danny added.

Michelle gave her father a big hug. "Thanks, Dad."

"You're welcome, sweetie," Danny said. "Why don't you put your extra pets in the garage for now? I think that's a good, safe place for them."

"Okay, Daddy," Michelle said.

Michelle and her friends placed the bunny, the parrot, and the snake in the garage. They played with the animals and gave them some food. Then they raced back to Michelle's room to feed her guinea pig.

Michelle scooped her pet out of his cage and handed him to Mandy. Then she poured some guinea pig food into a small bowl.

"So what are you going to name him?" Mandy asked, petting the guinea pig's shiny black fur.

"Hmmmm," Michelle replied. "I'm not sure." She picked up a celery stick from inside the cage and held it out to her pet.

"Well, at least we have time to think about it now," Cassie said.

Michelle nodded, watching the animal chomp on the vegetable. "That's right," she said. "Now that I have only *one* pet to worry about."

"I know!" Mandy said suddenly. "Let's call him—"

Ding-dong!

"Michelle!" Danny called from downstairs. "There's someone here to see you!"

"I wonder who it is," Michelle said.

Michelle, Cassie, and Mandy bounded down the stairs to see who was at the door. A girl with blond hair, holding a little yellow kitten, was standing in the living room.

"Hi, Michelle," the girl said. "You don't know me, but last Friday Lucas Hamilton told me you were looking for a pet and . . ."

"Oh, no!" Michelle cried. "Not again!"